Magically Winnie!

Wilbur

Winnie the Witch

Wayne

Wanda

The Shopkeeper

Uncle Owen

Mrs Parmar

Jerry the Giant

Cousin Cuthbert

Auntie Alice

Nigel

The Merman

The Little Ordinaries

The Head Teacher

OXFORD
UNIVERSITY PRESS

Great Clarendon Street, Oxford OX2 6DP

Oxford University Press is a department of the University of Oxford.
It furthers the University's objective of excellence in research, scholarship,
and education by publishing worldwide in

Oxford New York

Auckland Cape Town Dar es Salaam Hong Kong Karachi
Kuala Lumpur Madrid Melbourne Mexico City Nairobi
New Delhi Shanghai Taipei Toronto

With offices in
Argentina Austria Brazil Chile Czech Republic France Greece
Guatemala Hungary Italy Japan Poland Portugal Singapore
South Korea Switzerland Thailand Turkey Ukraine Vietnam

Oxford is a registered trade mark of Oxford University Press
in the UK and in certain other countries

British Library Cataloguing in Publication Data
Data available

ISBN: 978-0-19-273464-8 (paperback)

2 4 6 8 10 9 7 5 3 1

Printed in Great Britain

Paper used in the production of this book is a natural, recyclable product made
from wood grown in sustainable forests. The manufacturing process conforms
to the environmental regulations of the country of origin

Laura Owen and Korky Paul

Magically Winnie!

OXFORD
UNIVERSITY PRESS

Contents

Winnie's Giant Party   9

The Abominable Winnie   31

Winnie's Mouse Organ   55

Winnie takes the Plunge   77

Ssshh! Winnie   99

Flipping Winnie   121

Winnie's Sat Nav   145

Winnie Shapes Up   167

Winnie's House Party   189

Winnie's Pedal Power   211

Winnie Minds the Baby   235

Winnie Goes for Gold   257

And Finally . . .   278

Winnie's Giant Party

'Hoo-bloomingray!' sang Winnie. 'It's the fancy dress party today!'

Winnie and Wilbur were taking a basket of food to the school ready for the party. They had pickle buns, and sandwiches with real sand in them.

'We've all got to dress up,' said Winnie. 'You can be Puss in Boots, Wilbur, and I'll be . . .' But Winnie wasn't looking where she was going.

Trip-crash!

9

'Oi!' said Winnie. 'What's that blooming log . . . er . . . leg . . . doing across the path?'

A muffled sound of deep sobbing came from the bushes beside the path.

Sob!

'Jerry?' said Winnie. 'Is that you?'

Sniff! 'Yes, missus,' said Jerry.

Winnie pushed through the bush.

'What in the whoopsy-world is up with you?' said Winnie.

'It's just—sniff—that there's a party . . . !'

'I know!' said Winnie. 'Everyone's invited!'

'. . . except me!' said Jerry.

'Why's that, then?' said Winnie.

'Cos I is a giant!' said Jerry. 'Everybody's read giant stories in books, and now they think all giants is 'orrible. That's why I'm not invited!'

'Rubbish bins!' said Winnie. 'There are some lovely stories about giants. There's that nice one about Jack climbing up the beansprout where he meets a giant who . . . ooer. Well, there's that one about the Shellfish Giant who doesn't let the children . . . oh. I do see what you mean, Jerry!' said Winnie. 'But that's just blooming stories, not real life and people like us!'

'Then how come nobody ever wants to play with me?' said Jerry.

'Wilbur and I will!' said Winnie. 'Come on, let's play hide and sneak. Go and hide, Jerry. I'll count to a hundred, then I'll come and find you.'

'Goody!' smiled Jerry, and off he went—thump, thump, thump!

Winnie began to count.

'One nitty-gnat, two nitty-gnat, three nitty-gnat . . .'

Thump, thump, thump!

'Go quietly!' shouted Winnie. 'I can hear where you are! Twenty-two nitty-gnat, twenty- . . .'

Tiptoe-crash! Tiptoe-crack!

'Ninety-eight nitty-gnat, ninety-nine nitty gnat, *one hundred!*' shouted Winnie. 'Coming, ready-steady or not!'

14

Winnie opened her eyes . . . and saw
Jerry's bottom sticking right out of the
smelly-berry bush . . . just at the same
moment as a little girl saw it, and . . .

Shriek! 'Where'th my Mumumummy?'
shouted the little girl.

'Er, found you, Jerry!' said Winnie.

'See, missus!' said Jerry. 'See?
I ain't no good at playing!
And I frighten people!'

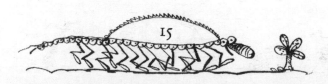

15

'You've turned hide and sneak into hide and shriek!' said Winnie. 'Let's try leapfrog instead!'

Thump-bump! went Winnie as she tried to leap over Jerry but leapt into him instead. **Splat!** went Wilbur. Jerry was just too big for them to get over.

'Oo, I'm as puffed as popcorn and as bruised as a boomerang banana!' said Winnie. 'I give up!'

'See?' said Jerry. 'See?'

'Yes, I do see,' said Winnie. 'But don't you worry, Jerry! You *shall* go to the party!'

Wilbur found an idea in a book of photos. It showed a street party from the olden days.

'Perfect!' said Winnie. 'Quick! I must phone Mrs Parmar!'

Down on the High Street, Winnie
waved her wand. 'Abracadabra!'

Instantly there was a ring road to take
all the cars away from the village. 'We
need party decorations,' said Winnie.
She waved her wand. 'Abracadabra!'
And there were flowers. 'I'll just put
them in pots,' said Winnie. She jumped

18

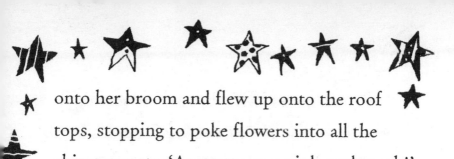

onto her broom and flew up onto the roof tops, stopping to poke flowers into all the chimney pots. 'As pretty as a pink cockroach!' she said. Then Winnie flew around, scooping up washing lines from back gardens to drape them from the lamp posts. 'Big bloomers bunting!' she said.

19

Down below, Mrs Parmar was sorting the tables and chairs and food and drink.

'Where can we put Jerry?' said Mrs Parmar. 'He'd break any of these ordinary chairs!'

'Leave it to me, Mrs P!' said Winnie. '*Abracadabra!*'

Instantly there was a giant throne of a chair. And there was a hole in the ground so that Jerry's chair could be sunk down and be at the right height for him to use the same table as everyone else.

'Well done, Winnie!' said Mrs Parmar. She laid Jerry a place with a dustbin lid plate and a bucket cup.

'Here they all come!' said Mrs Parmar. 'We'll have party games first, then tea. Oh, but we're not dressed-up, Winnie!'

'Easy-peasy tight pants squeezy!' said Winnie. She waved her wand.

Abradacabra!

21

Don't Winnie and Mrs Parmar look
lovely?

Mrs Parmar announced the first party
game.

'Hide and Seek!'

'Dear, oh dear, Wilbur!' said Winnie.
'How's Jerry going to get on? Where is he,
anyway?'

Wilbur shrugged.

The children hid here and there, and
just about everywhere. Some of them
chose to hide in a tree. They climbed up
into its branches, then they sat and waited
to be found.

'I like it up here!' said one child.

'So do I,' said another, 'Did you know that Jerry the giant is coming to the party?'

The tree quivered.

'Is he?' said a third child. 'Oh, good! I like Jerry.'

'So do I!' said both the other children. Then—**splash!**—'What's that?' said the first one. 'It's raining inside this tree!'

But it wasn't rain. It was Jerry.

'Sniff!' went the tree.

'Jerry?' said Winnie. 'Is that you?'

'It is, missus!' said Jerry. **'I is crying because I is so happy!'**

'Jerry's costume wins the fancy dress competition!' said Mrs Parmar. 'He's a wonderful tree! He gets a book for his prize.'

'Oo, just a moment, Mrs P,' said Winnie when she saw the book in Mrs Parmar's hand. She waved her wand. *Abracadabra!'*

Instantly the book changed.

'Is it a book about giants?' asked Jerry, looking worried.

'Yes, but NICE giants!' said Winnie.

'Ooo,' said Jerry, and he hugged the book hard.

Jerry let the children climb all over him, and he swung them round.

Then, 'Shall we play leapfrog?' said
Winnie.

'But . . . !' began Jerry.

'Don't worry!' said Winnie. She waved
her wand. *Abracadabra!*

27

And instantly all the children had froggy legs and froggy feet. They could leap over Jerry with no trouble at all.

Leap! Leap! Leap!

But when it was Jerry's turn to leap over the children, they all collapsed!

'Time for tea!' said Mrs Parmar.

They ate and they talked. Then they filled the hole in the ground with water, and the children went swimming with their froggy legs which made them swim extra fast!

And guess what? When Jerry got home he found an invitation stuck in his letter box. He'd been invited to the party all along, but just didn't know it!

'You silly great lummox!' said Winnie.

INVITATION to Jerry

The Abominable Winnie!

Winnie looked out of the window and squealed.

'Yippeee-dippeee, Wilbur! There's snow as deep as a maggoty-mallow pie!'

Winnie went down to the kitchen and made a big blubbling bucket of grey splorridge. She dolloped the splorridge into mini cauldrons, then dribbled it with snail syrup.

'Mmmm!' said Winnie. Sniff! 'That smells truly abominable!'

31

'Meeow?' asked Wilbur, licking syrup off his spoon.

'D'you like that word—abominable?' said Winnie. 'I'm not completely absolutely sure what it means, but I have been told that my cooking is abominable.' **Lick! Slurp!**

'**Yum!** So abominable must mean really, really, really nice, mustn't it?'

'Meeow!' Wilbur shook his head and pointed towards a dictionary, but Winnie was looking out of the window.

'Let's go out and play!'

They put on hats and gloves and tail warmers, and went out into the cold.

33

'Watch this!' said Winnie. **Splodge!**
She tipped herself over into the snow to
make a witch-shaped print. It was a bit
messy.

Splat! Wilbur made a cat print that
was crisp and clean. He added twigs for
whiskers.

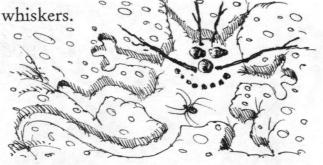

'I s'ppose yours is better!' said Winnie.
They made an ice slide, and slid along it
with their arms out to help them balance
Wheeeeeeee-bump! went Winnie.
Wheeeeeeeeeeeeeee! went
Wilbur, going much further.

'Huh!' said Winnie, rubbing her bottom.
'Snowball fights are what I'm really really—
abominably—good at. Watch this!' Winnie
scooped up snow and squashed it into
a ball. She threw the snowball at
Wilbur—*splat!*

35

'Splat on the cat!' said Winnie. 'Hee hee!'

Plop! Wilbur threw one back, and soon they were having a snowball fight.

Chuck! went Winnie. **Splat!**

'Hit!'

'Mrrrow!'

Throw! went Wilbur. **Duck!** went Winnie.

'Missed!' shouted Winnie.

Then Wilbur scooped a really big
snowball and threw it—**pheeeew-plop!**
to land wetly and coldly right down
Winnie's neck.

'Urgh!' shouted Winnie. 'Ooo, you
meany, Wilbur! That was horrible.'

'Meeheehee!' laughed Wilbur.

'Stop it!' said Winnie. 'Or I'm not playing with you any more!'

But Wilbur threw another snowball that landed—**splat!**—right in Winnie's face.

'Meeheehee!'

'Right!' said Winnie. 'You're not my friend any more, Wilbur the cat!'

Winnie stomped off to where the children were making snowmen.

'Can I help?' asked Winnie.

She added this . . . and that . . . and those
to make the snowman more special. 'Good,
isn't it!' said Winnie.

'Look at that one!' laughed the children.
They were pointing to where Wilbur had
made another snowman. 'It's a snow witch!
Snow Winnie! Ha ha!'

'Huh!' said Winnie. 'I can make our snowman better than that one! Shall I?'

'Yes, please!' said the children.

'I'll make it into an abominable snowman!' said Winnie. She waved her wand.

'Abracadabra!'

'Uh-oh!' said the children. 'W-w-what's that?'

'A lovely abominable snowman, that's what,' said Winnie. 'A really nice big . . . Er, it really is very very big, isn't it!'

Gulp! went the children.

The abominable snowman was *huge!* It was hairy. And it was moving! It was taking great big footsteps towards them, and it didn't look friendly! **Thump-thump!**

'Er, hello, nice Mr Abominable!' said
Winnie.

THUMP-THUMP!

'Heck in a hairnet, run!' shouted
Winnie. Winnie and the children began
to run down the hill, but the abominable
snowman was running even faster after
them.

Thump-thump-thump!

'He's going to catch us!' said Winnie.

Dive! Wilbur threw himself at the
abominable snowman, trying to stop it.
But the abominable snowman just tripped
over Wilbur and began to roll down the
hill, roly-poly faster and faster, turning
itself into a giant snowball.

Rumble-roll!

'*Abraca*——!' began Winnie. But **splat-gulp!** Winnie was rolled into the ball that was growing bigger and bigger as it picked up more snow. The abominable snowball began to pick up children too. **Splat-gulp! Splat-gulp!**

Then, 'Leave those children alone, you great bully!' shouted Mrs Parmar. She stepped into the path of the abominable snowman that had turned into an abominable snowball. She held up a hand—

'Stop!' she commanded. But the abominable snowball scooped up Mrs Parmar, too.

Luckily the hill flattened out, so the abominable snowball rolled to a halt. There were arms, legs and heads sticking out of it.

44

'Frosted fidgets!' said Winnie. 'Where's my wand?' Wilbur ran up and handed her the wand. She just managed to wave it. *Abracadabra!*

Ppffuff! The snowball gently exploded, spilling Winnie and children and Mrs Parmar into the snow. The abominable snowman snowball was gone.

'Thank snow goosey-ganders for that!' said Winnie. She tried to stand up, but fell straight over because she was so dizzy from rolling. But she was smiling. 'Eee, I've just had a blooming brilliant idea!' she said.

'Oh dear,' said dizzy Mrs Parmar.

'We should make a really big snow ball!' said Winnie.

'Absolutely *not* another one!' said Mrs Parmar. 'We've all had quite enough of big snowballs for one day.'

'Not a snowball, Mrs P!' said Winnie. 'A Snow Ball! You know, with dancing and posh frocks and bow ties and music and all that!'

But Mrs Parmar was still shaking her head. 'We couldn't possibly organize a snow ball by this evening. There isn't time to make food and buy dresses and . . .'

'Just look over there, everybody!' said Winnie. All the heads turned, and Winnie gave a quick whisk of her wand.
'Abracadabra!'

'Wow!'

Instantly there was a sparkling snow dome made from the abominable snowball's snow. An igloo ballroom! And everyone was dressed for a ball. There was a band. And food. And balloons.

Doo-be-doo-wap-wap! The music started.

'Ahem, meeeow!'

'Wilbur!' said Winnie. 'Oh, you look so dashing! And you were so brave, trying to save us from that abominable snowman!'

'Meeow!' said Wilbur modestly.

'Oh, Wilbur, I'm sorry I was as moody as a mouldy melon earlier!' said Winnie. 'Please, can we be friends again?'

'Meeow!' grinned Wilbur. He held up
one front leg.

'Ooo, yes! I'd love to dance with you!'
said Winnie.

So Winnie and Wilbur, and Mrs Parmar
and all the children, danced as the night
grew dark outside. They danced as the sun
began to rise and warm the world, and the
igloo ballroom began to drip.

Everyone was hot from dancing.

'*Abracadabra!*' said Winnie, and suddenly the snow of the ballroom turned into red and orange and green and purple ice-lollies.

'Have a lick!' said Winnie.

Winnie licked green gherkin lolly while Wilbur munched on a golden kipper-flavoured chunk.

'You know what, Wilbur?' said Winnie. 'That was an abominable party!'

'You're wrong, Winnie!' said Mrs Parmar. 'Abominable means terrible.'

'Does it?' said Winnie.

'And that party was wonderful!'

'So my abominable cooking is . . .'

'*Interesting,*' said Mrs Parmar firmly. 'Goodbye!'

Winnie's Mouse Organ

Pong! Phew!

Winnie and Wilbur were flying along with pegs on their noses because they'd got some lumps of the smelliest green hairy mouldy cheese in their basket.

'This will tempt those blooming noisy mice out!' said Winnie. 'I'll put it in the crocodile jaw trap, and it can **snip-snap** them up, and then tonight we can sleep! We won't be woken by their blooming scratching and squeaking ever again!'

Then, 'Ooo, look at that, Wilbur!' said
Winnie. There was a poster outside the
school. 'Just look at that shiny snaily
thingy! And a great big nappy pin!
Whatever are they?'

Mrs Parmar was coming out of the
school.

Sniff! 'What's that ghastly smell?' she asked.

'Just cheese,' said Winnie. 'Do you want to try some?'

'No thank you!' said Mrs Parmar. 'Ah! I see that you're looking at our poster. We are hoping to enthuse the children with a love of music.'

'Coo!' said Winnie. 'I'm enthused already! I'd love to play one of those funny things!'

'Well,' said Mrs Parmar. 'If you could play an instrument, you would be more than welcome at school this afternoon. So far we haven't been able to find a musician to come and play for us.'

'Ooo, I'll volunteer, Mrs P!' said Winnie. 'I'll show the little ordinaries how to make lovely music!'

'Mrrrow!' Wilbur dropped his head into his paws.

'Which instrument do you play?' asked Mrs Parmar.

'Oh,' said Winnie. 'It's . . . er . . . um. Well, you'll just have to wait and see, Mrs P. But I'll be along later with my ninstrument, don't you worry!'

'Well, thank you!' said Mrs Parmar. 'I'll tell the head teacher right away!'

'Wow-zow!' said Winnie, as they
flew home. 'Ooo, lovely-dovely
brillaramaroodles! I'm going to be
a musician!'

'Meeeow?' asked Wilbur.

'How?' said Winnie. 'Easy-peasy
turnip-juice-squeezy! I just need a
ninstrument and then I'll play it.'

Back home, Winnie waved her wand.

Abracadabra!

And instantly, there at Winnie's feet was something that looked like a hairy beast with spikes.

'Hisss!' went Wilbur.

'It's a blagpipe!' said Winnie. 'Just you listen to this!' Winnie blew down a pipe. Up plumped the hairy balloony bag. Then a terrible high-up **waiiiiiiil** came from the pipes.

'Hiss!' **Pounce! Pop! Waiiiiil** . . .

'Oh, Wilbur, you've squashed it!' said Winnie. 'What did you do that for? I'll have to try another ninstrument.' Winnie held her wand end on to her lips.
Abracadabra!

In an instant, Winnie had a shiny trumpet in her hands.

'Lovely! I'll do a fanflare!'

Winnie blew.

No noise came out.

Wilbur smiled. He relaxed.

Winnie scowled and blew a raspberry
down the trumpet. **Paaarp!**
Paaarp-paaarp!

Wilbur pulled a cushion over his head.
PAAAARP! went Winnie.
'Mrrrow!' wailed Wilbur.

'Oh, blooming heck, Wilbur! Perhaps
I should try something quieter. Perhaps
a stringy thingy ninstrument.' Winnie
waved her wand like a bow.
'Abracadabra!'

And there was a violin. Winnie lifted
the violin to her chin, then she began to
stroke the bow over the strings—
screeeeech.

'Mrrrow-ow-ow!' screeched Wilbur,
even louder.

'You'll have to go outside!' said Winnie.
'I can't learn a ninstrument with you
making that kind of a racket! Out you
go and leave me to perfectify my music-
playing in time for school!'

Winnie threw Wilbur out. Slam! She shut the door on him.

'**Squeak-tee-hee!**' laughed the mice who were peeping around corners. They'd been sniffing that cheese, but not daring to come out while Wilbur was there. Now . . .

'**Squeak!**' Sniff-sniff! Scuttle-scuttle!

Out came mice from every corner and crevice of the house.

'Go away!' said Winnie as one scuttled over her foot. 'Get off!' Winnie kicked.

'Squeak!' went the mouse.

'Oh!' said Winnie. 'That was a nice little sound!' She gently poked another mouse with her wand.

'Squeak!'

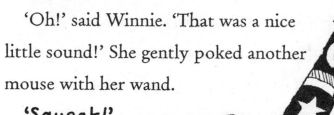

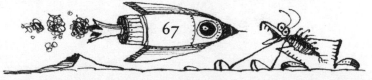

'What a lovely low squeak!' she said. 'Hmm. I've just had a blooming good idea!'

Winnie tiptoed to the door and quietly opened it. **Creeeeak!** 'Wilbur!' she whispered. 'Come back inside and catch some mice for me, but don't hurt them!'

In came Wilbur. Soon he'd got eight different-sized mice, and put them in a box.

'Right,' said Winnie. 'Time to go off to the school!'

In the school hall all the little ordinaries
sat nice and quiet, waiting to see what Winnie
had in her box. So did the teachers. So did
Mrs Parmar. Up went one small hand.

'What kind of an instrument is it?'

'It's a mouse organ!' said Winnie. 'Shall
I show you?'

'Yes please!' shouted all the little
ordinaries.

So Winnie opened the box. She tipped
out the mice. The mice looked a bit shy.
Winnie put them in size order, then she
gave one a gentle prod with her finger.

'**Squeak!**' went the mouse.

Giggle! went the children.

Winnie poked another. '**Squeak!**'
And another. '**Squeak!**'

'Um . . . is that it?' asked Mrs Parmar.
'Just mice squeaking?'

'Er . . .' said Winnie. But Wilbur was handing her her wand.

'Oh, no!' said Mrs Parmar, holding up a hand. 'Absolutely no magic in front of the children!'

'I was only going to conduct the mice with my baton,' said Winnie.

'Oh, very well, then,' said Mrs Parmar.

71

Winnie raised her wand. She pretended
to cough but she was actually
cough-whispering, 'Abracadabra!'

And instantly . . .

'We are eight little mice

Squeak-squeak!

Who live in Winnie's hice

Squeak-squeak!

And sing very nice.

72

In winter when it's cold
If we're feeling bold
We'll slide down the ice-icles.
Squeak-squeak!

In summer when it's hot
We really like a lot
To ride on our bice-icles.
Squeak-squeak!'

73

The children laughed and clapped, and
they were soon singing and squeaking
along too. The teachers were delighted.

'Phew in a shrew stew!' said Winnie to
Wilbur as they left the school. 'And
nobody noticed the magic, did they?'

Back home, they opened up the box of mice, and now, instead of Winnie feeling cross with the mice and Wilbur feeling greedy for the mice, they felt all soppy about the mice.

'Shall we all share some cheese?' said Winnie.

'Meeow,' nodded Wilbur.

So the mice joined them for a pongy cheese party before they all settled into bed.

'Sweet cheesy dreams, everyone!' yawned Winnie. Then they all lay awake all night.

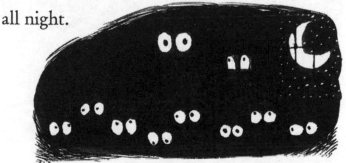

75

Winnie takes the Plunge

Gurgle! went Winnie's loo. **Gurgle-wurgle!**

Winnie pulled the handle again, but it wouldn't flush! It just went **belch-burp!**

'Oh, leaping loo rolls!' said Winnie. 'There's something wrong with this blooming loo, and I don't know what to do about it!'

'Meeow?' suggested Wilbur, waving a plunger.

'It's worth a try!' agreed Winnie.

Splish-splosh! Squirt! Squelch!
went the plunger. Winnie pulled the
handle again. **Burp!** went the loo.

'There's something down there!' said
Winnie. 'Something getting in the way!'
She leant over the loo, peering deep down
into the bowl. 'Pull the handle, Wilbur,
and I'll see if I can see what's blocking it.'

Yank! went Wilbur on the handle.
And **flush-swoosh!** went the loo.

'Ahhhh!' went Winnie as she was
flushed down the pan.

'Mrrow!'

Wilbur tried to hold on to Winnie's
legs. But the pent-up flush was so fierce it
swept Winnie down and away.

Βικτωρια
ΦΑΛΛΣ

79

'Meeeow!' cried Wilbur. 'Meow, meow!'
But the loo was empty. Winnie was gone.
'Meeow!' wailed Wilbur in a voice he
hadn't used since he was a kitten.

Down the pipes Winnie was whizzing—
whoops! whoops!—just as if she was
going down a flume at the swimming pool.
Except this pipe was dark. This pipe was
smelly. This pipe went on and on . . .

Gasp! went Winnie, coming up for
air but still swishing along. 'What the
blooming . . . ?' Something slimy and
wiggly was swimming along with her.
'Who in the loo are you? Are you the
loo-blocking critter?' said Winnie. She gave
the critter a good poke with her wand as
she struggled on down the pipe.

Winnie was running out of energy for swimming. Help! thought Winnie. Splashing and gurgling, she just about managed to wave her wand. If you've tried waving anything under water you'll know that it isn't as easy as it is in the air. But Winnie pushed her wand in a slow swish. '*Abra-gurgle-cadabra!*' And instantly Winnie's legs were transformed into a mermaid tail!

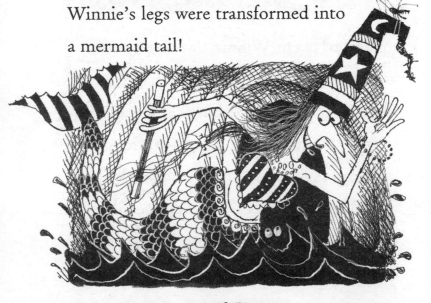

She waggled her tail, and shot-swam through the water.

'Wheee!' said Winnie. And—**sploosh!**—out she squirted from the pipe into clear cold salty water that glittered brightly in the sunshine. Wiggle-waggle went Winnie's tail, pushing her upwards towards air and light and . . .

'Where the blooming heck am I?' said soggy Winnie.

'You, my dear, are in Merland!' said a deep voice. And there in the water beside Winnie was a handsome merman, flipping his handsome tail.

'Oooer!' said Winnie. 'Er . . . could you tell me which direction is home, please?'

'Certainly! You will come home with me, my dear!' said the merman. 'You can be my merwife!' And he placed a string of pearls around Winnie's neck.

'Ooo, no. No thank you!' said Winnie.
'But I am strong and brave. You must
marry me!' The merman took hold of
Winnie's arm.

Winnie bopped the merman on the
head with her wand, but he snatched it
from her. 'Let go, you blooming bully!'
said Winnie. 'Anyway, I bet you're not as
brave as my Wilbur is! He'll be here soon.'

'Wilbur?' said the merman. 'Is Wilbur
your big brother?'

'No! He's my cat!' said Winnie. 'He'll
be coming to rescue me, I'm sure. Look!
I think that's him now!'

Now, if there's one thing fishy people
are scared of, it's cats. 'I'm off!' said the
merman, and away he dived.

A small dot on the horizon was getting bigger as it got closer. 'Wilbur!' shouted Winnie. Wilbur was on an old plank, trying to paddle with a wooden spoon. 'Oh, Wilbur, you're as brave as twenty mermen! Take me home, Wilbur!'

Winnie powered the raft through the water with her wonderful tail.

'This tail is brillaramaroodles for swimming,' said Winnie. 'But when we get home I'm going to need to magic my legs back.' But just then . . . 'Whoops!' Winnie was caught up in a fisherman's net and hauled aboard his boat.

'Mrrrow!' protested Wilbur.

'Oi!' shouted Winnie.

But the fisherman had his iCod on and didn't hear a thing.

When they reached the harbour,
Winnie was thrown into a van with the
other fish. Wilbur clung to the back as
they drove to the fish shop. But he
couldn't stop Winnie from being
dumped onto the counter.

'Meeow!' said Wilbur, as Winnie floundered with the flounders and the chip shop man beat up his batter. 'Meeeow!'

'Throw some fish heads to that noisy cat!' said the fish-and-chip shop man.

Wilbur kept banging on the window and pointing, but, 'I'm not giving you that big cross fish, if that's what you're after!' laughed the fish-and-chip shop man.

The man peeled the potatoes to make
chips, and he lit the stove. It wouldn't
be long before he began cooking the fish.
So, as fast as a blast, Wilbur ran to Jerry's
house. There he told Scruff . . .

'Meeow meow-meow!'

'Ruff-woof!' agreed Scruff.

Then Scruff told Jerry, so Jerry came running, with Scruff and Wilbur trying to keep up, all the way back to the fish-and-chip shop.

Jerry stomped into the fish shop. **'I wants a giant-sized fish and chips, please!'**

'*Giant-sized?*' said the fish-and-chip shop man.

'Aha! We do have an exceptionally large fish in the catch today. I'll just pop it into the fryer.'

'No!'

'Mrrrow!'

'Woof!'

'Er . . . I likes my fish raw,' said Jerry.

'Really?' said the fish-and-chip shop man. 'Well, that saves me a job!' He piled a mountain of chips onto a huge bit of paper, then he plonked Winnie on top of the chips.

'Fanks!' said Jerry. His fish-and-chip parcel was wriggling and saying rude things. So he sat on some grass and unwrapped his supper. His 'fish' had her hands on her hips.

'Why didn't you stop him from showering me in blooming salt and vinegar?' asked Winnie. 'I feel as sour and as salty as a pickled bunion!'

But Winnie soon cheered up, scoffing chips. And Wilbur ran home to fetch a spare wand. Winnie waved it. *'Abracadabra!'*

And instantly her legs were back.

'Oo, that's blooming better!' said Winnie. 'Legs are useful!'

They walked home as the sun set.

'I'll mend your loo, if you like,' offered Jerry.

'Oo, would you?' said Winnie.

So Jerry brought his mallet, and **smash!**—that was the end of the problem loo.

'But now we haven't got *any* loo!' said Winnie. 'Heck, where's that wand? **Abracadabra!'**

And there was a pair of loos. His and hers. Winnie and Wilbur pulled down a handle each.

Flush! Flush! No problem.

'Hoo-blooming-ray' said Winnie.

Ssshh! Winnie

There was only a murmur of polite
conversation in the shop . . . until Winnie
came in, barging her way like a rampaging
rhinoceros. **Crash!** She had red spots all
over her, and she was scratching at them.

Itch, itch! 'Ooo, I'm as itchy as
a witchy in a ditchy full of itching
powder!' said Winnie. **Trip! Crump!**
She knocked over a display. 'Sorry!'
shouted Winnie. There was a queue for the
counter, but Winnie shoved to the front.

Itch, scratch! ' 'Scuse me!' she shouted. 'I need just one incy little ingredient so that I can make a pepper gherkin potion to get rid of my rash. I'll be as quick as a lick on a lolly stick, I promise! Mr Shopkeeper, have you got a jar of knobbly pickled gherkins and a chilli pepper or two?'

'Well, really!' huffed Mrs Parmar. 'All this noise is most unnecessary! You should join our sponsored silence at school, Winnie!'

'A sponsored what?' asked Winnie.

'Silence,' said Mrs Parmar pulling a leaflet out of her bag. 'You get people to pay you for every minute that you can keep absolutely quiet.'

'Coo!' said Winnie.

'The money goes to the poorest children in the world,' said Mrs Parmar.

'Double coo like a blooming pair of doves!' said Winnie. 'I'll do that for those poor little ordinaries!'

'Ha! You'll never keep quiet!' said
the shopkeeper. The other customers all
laughed at the idea as well.

'I blooming well will!' humphed
Winnie. 'I can keep quiet for, oh, ever
so long!'

'Do it now, then!' said Mrs Parmar.

'All right!' said Winnie.

'Tee-hee! Ha-ha!' went everybody.
'You just said something!'

'That's not flip-flapping fair!' said
Winnie. 'If you promise me money to be
quiet, then I'll keep as quiet as a fossil with
a gag on, you'll see!'

So they all promised to pay Winnie to
keep quiet, and she hurried home.

'Hey, Wilbur,' said Winnie. 'I'm going
to keep quiet for the poorest little
ordinaries in the world.'

'Me-heow!' wondered Wilbur.

'I will!' said Winnie. **Itch!** 'Now, please help me make that potion, Wilbur. If I can just stop this itching I'll be calm and quiet and make lots of money!'

So Wilbur mashed gherkins **squelch!**— and Winnie bashed peppercorns— **crunch!**—and they popped in the chillis and blitzed it all in a mangle-masher— **bzzzbzzzbzz!**—and out came some green gloop.

Winnie slopped the gloop into her hand
and slapped it all over her face.

'There! Have the spots gone?' asked
Winnie. Wilbur pointed to the mirror.
Winnie looked, and put her hands to her
cheeks. 'Heck, the spots have turned blue!'
Then she gasped and gasped again—
'Ah-ah-tishoo!'

'Meeow?' asked Wilbur.

105

'I-I-I've got the sn-sn-sneeezes!' wailed
Winnie. **'Ah-ah-tishoo!** And blue
spots! Something's not right!'

Wilbur went to the computer and
clicked the mouse to find the 'symptoms
and their causes' website.

Wilbur typed in 'blue spots' and
'sneezes'.

Click! The computer spoke the result.

'These symptoms are indicative
of an allergic reaction to
a surfeit of pepper.'

'Oh, no!' wailed Winnie.

'But that's too late!' wailed Winnie.

'Ah-ah-tishoo. I've got to keep quiet for the sponsored silence! **Ah-ah-tishoo.** Today!'

Wilbur brought Winnie a hot drink of warm parsnip juice.

'**Ah-ah-tishoo.**'

He brought her a hot warty bottle.

'**Ah-ah-tishoo.** Heck in a hankie, nothing ... **ah-tishoo** ... is going to work!' said Winnie.

So Wilbur brought Winnie her wand.

'Oh, of course! Silly me!' said Winnie. '**Ah-ah-tishoo.** *Abracadabra!*'

And instantly, there was a bottle with
a seething pink liquid in it, and a large
spoon. Winnie took a spoonful of pink
stuff, then made a face . . . Then there was
silence. The sneezing had stopped.

'Hoo-blooming-ray!' said Winnie.
Then . . .

Hic! Hic-hic!

'Oh, flipping noodles!' said Winnie. **'Hic!** Now I've got hiccups that won't **hic! hic!** stop. However am I going to keep quiet?'

'Blleeugh! Hissss!' went Wilbur to give Winnie a shock.

'Yikes, Wilbur, you made me jump like a flea in a frying pan!' But ... silence ... the hiccups had gone.

'Yay!' said Winnie. 'Let's go!'

Down in the school hall everyone
looked surprised when Winnie
walked in.

'Ooer, with all that hiccup fun I'd
forgotten about the spots!' said Winnie.

III

But the little ordinaries and Winnie all
sat down and put fingers to their lips.

'Now,' said Mrs Parmar. 'We will count
down to absolute silence. Five, four, three,
two, one!'

Silence . . . until, **'Hic!'** went Winnie.

Winnie clamped a hand over her mouth,
but she couldn't hold them in. **Hic! hic!**

'Disqualified!' boomed Mrs Parmar so loudly that Winnie jumped as high as a kangaroo on a trampoline . . . and the hiccups were properly gone!

'Oo, ooo, please let me try again!' said Winnie. 'For the sake of those poor little ordinaries?'

'Oh, I suppose so,' said Mrs Parmar. 'Five, four, three, two, one . . .'

Silence. Tick, tock, tick, tock. Silence for a minute. Winnie rested her head on the table. Tick, tock, tick, tock. Silence for half a minute more . . . then:

Snooooore. GRUNT!! Sn-sn-snooore!

'Disqualified!' whispered Mrs Parmar. Wilbur put his head in his paws.

The little ordinaries kept quiet for minutes and minutes, but then they were beginning to get bored . . . until something wonderful happened. Winnie started to talk her dream . . .

' . . . Wilbur the panther stalks his walk
and talks to a teasing monkey in a tree . . .
and that monkey is me! And I'm flying on
a banana—wheeee! Up to where my wings
flip-flap fly me to the big silver moon . . .
that's a pool of deep water, and in I dive . . .'

The little ordinaries sat in silence,
listening to the mumble of dream as an hour
and more passed. The words tumbled and
the clock tick-tocked and on Winnie
went . . . 'So we make sandwiches of leaves
and bugs and pepper, lots of pepper, and
I sniff and . . .'

Winnie suddenly sat up, looking
startled. **'Ah-ah-ah!'** she went.
'Ah-ah-atishooo!' And off shot her
blue spots . . . to land on Mrs Parmar.

'Ha ha ha!' laughed the little ordinaries.

Brrrrp! went Mrs Parmar's whistle.
'Disqualified, all of you! The sponsored
silence is at an end!' said Mrs Parmar.

'Uh-oh! Was that my flipping fault?' asked Winnie.

'In a way,' said Mrs Parmar. 'But you kept the children beautifully quiet for far longer than they could ever have lasted without your dream story to keep them entertained. The children have raised lots of money, and I thank you for that, Winnie.'

'Oh, goody three shoes,' said Winnie.
'Um. Don't worry about the spots, Mrs P.
They'll be gone in twenty-four hours or
sooner if you have a good sneeze.'

'What spots?' said Mrs Parmar.

But Winnie and Wilbur were already
on their way home.

119

Flipping Winnie

'It's a blooming lovely spring day!' said Winnie, hopping on one leg as she tugged-up a boot lace. 'The sun's shining, grass is growing, flowers are flowering, lambs and funny rabbits are hopping, and . . . er . . . and there's something very strange walking up the drive.' Winnie peered further out of the window.

'Meeow?'

'No, silly me, it's only Mrs Parmar! Whatever in the witchy world does she want?'

121

Snap! 'Oh, my blooming bootlace has broken!'

Winnie shiffle-shuffled to the front door.

'Good morning, Winnie,' said Mrs Parmar. 'Did you know that today is Spring Fair Day?' Mrs Parmar glanced at Winnie's feet. 'They are giving away nice shoes as prizes, you know.'

122

'Ooo, just what I need!' said Winnie. 'What do I do to win a pair?'

'Well, there's a pancake competition,' said Mrs Parmar.

'Pancakes?' said Winnie. 'Easy-peasy squashed-slug squeezy! My cowpat pancakes are famous!'

Mrs Parmar made a face. 'You'd have to make a normal kind of pancake for racing.'

123

VA-VROOOoM!

'Racing?' said Winnie. 'Do the pancakes
work as wheels, then?'

'No, no,' said Mrs Parmar. 'You run,
holding your frying pan with a pancake in
it, and while you run you keep tossing the
pancake up into the air so that it flips over
and lands on the other side.'

'That's sounds fun!' said Winnie. 'Are
you racing, Mrs P?'

124

Mrs Parmar shook her head. 'I've never won any prize in my entire life, so there's really no point.'

'That's as sad as a centipede with sore feet who can't find his soft slippers,' said Winnie. 'So how should I make a *normal* pancake?'

'Plain flour,' said Mrs Parmar. 'Eggs and milk. You mix them all together into a smooth batter, then pour the batter into a pan to cook.'

'Easy-sneezy!' said Winnie. 'See you at the Fair, then, Mrs P!'

Winnie shut the door. 'Right,' she said 'First I must do something about these blooming boots.'

'Meeow?' suggested Wilbur, offering a big jar with long black things curled inside.

'Liquorice laces—perfect!' said Winnie. She threaded two laces in and out of holes, then tied them. 'Brillaramaroodles! Now for the pancakes. What was the first ingredient Mrs P said? Flowers, wasn't it?'

126

127

So they went into the garden and
collected a whole basket-full of croakuses
and snowdrips and daffidoodles.

'We'd better bash them a bit, or they'll
never mix properly,' said Winnie. 'Ooo, I
almost forgot! Mrs P particularly said "plain
flower", so not those frilly daffidoodles.
Put those ones on one side, Wilbur.'

Bang-squelch, they pounded the flowers to a greeny-yellowy mush. 'Eggs next,' said Winnie.

Winnie found an old ostrich egg and Wilbur found a tangle of spider eggs. **Crack-splash-mix,** they broke the big egg and threw in the teeny-tiny eggs and mixed them all into the yellow-green mush.

129

'Now it just needs a splash of milk,' said
Winnie. She took a bottle of old skunk
milk from the fridge, and poured it in.

Wilbur held his nose.

Slop-whisk! 'Is that a "smooth
batter", Wilbur?'

He pointed a claw at the green lumps
floating in the goo.

'Well, it'll have to do,' said Winnie.
'Get that pan hot so that we can cook it.'

Sizzle-stick!

'Blooming heck!' said Winnie. She
scraped and scratched at the blobby green
pancake. 'At least it isn't runny. Come on,
Wilbur, we don't want to miss the race!'

Step went Winnie, **trip-splat!**

'Ouch! Now the blooming mice have eaten these laces!'

Wilbur handed Winnie her wand.

'Abracadabra!'

And instantly Winnie's boots were laced with skinny snakes. They hissed, and the mice ran off.

'Ready at last!' said Winnie.

They got down to the Spring Fair field just as the pancake-race contestants were lining up.

'Wait for me!' said Winnie, pushing her way in.

Brrrrrp! went the whistle. And they were off!

133

Some ran, some walked. Winnie ran past the choir conductor. Pancakes were being tossed up-twiddle-down all around her. Winnie was just running past the school dinner lady when . . .

'Meeow!' said Wilbur, and the head teacher bellowed through a megaphone. 'Anyone not tossing their pancake will be disqualified!'

'But my pancake is stuck!' shouted Winnie, 'It won't . . .' Then, **trip-twiddle-tumble!** Winnie's skinny snake laces had got bored so they slithered out of the boot holes. Because she was running, Winnie's trip made her somersault right over.

'See!' she panted, getting herself up onto her feet again. 'I flipped myself AND my pancake!'

'Doesn't count!' shouted the head teacher. 'The pancake must be tossed *out* of the pan!'

'Oh, nits' knickers!' muttered Winnie. She waved her wand. *Abracadabra!'*

This time Winnie's pancake *did* jump
out of her pan. Up-up-up-twiddle...
but it didn't come down.

'There's a new moon in the sky! A green
one!' said the head teacher. He clasped
his hands together. 'I've discovered a
new moon! They'll call it "Head Teacher
Moon" after me! I'll be famous!' He did
a little dance. 'I can retire!'

The head teacher gazed at the sky, and the race finished . . . and at last, **neeeeeow-flop!** Winnie's pancake fell back down . . . to land—**splat**—right on Mrs Parmar's head.

'Oh, whoopsy!' said Winnie. 'Sorry, Mrs P!' Winnie stepped forward to take the pancake off Mrs Parmar's head, but **trip-splat!** the boots did it again. 'Oh, mouldy maggots!' said Winnie. 'Let's get everything tied up securely once and for all.' She waved her wand. *'Abracadabra!'*

Instantly there was a whirl of wild
ribbons flying off the hats the children were
wearing for the best bonnet competition.
Winnie's boots were suddenly firmly tied
with a big red ribbon on the left boot,
a green one on her right. Wilbur had a
pink ribbon on his tail. Mrs Parmar had
a yellow ribbon tied under her chin,
securing the pancake firmly to her head.
The head teacher had a purple ribbon on his
megaphone.

'What a very strange day!' he said.
'Er . . . ladies and gentlemen, I had better
announce the winner of our best bonnet
competition.' The head teacher looked
towards the children whose ribbonless
bonnets were falling off their heads.
Then he saw Mrs Parmar.

Wilbur had tucked the daffidoodles into her pancake bonnet. 'Ah, Mrs Parmar!' said the head teacher. 'A picture of springtime beauty! You win the shoes!'

'Oh!' simpered Mrs Parmar.

'See, Mrs P?' said Winnie. 'I bet the only reason you've never won a competition before is that you've never entered one, have you?'

'Well, no I haven't,' agreed Mrs Parmar.

'But I think you should have these lovely
shoes, Winnie!'

'I don't need them now!' said Winnie,
pointing to her boots. 'So we're all happy.'

'Mrrrow!' complained Wilbur, who
was fighting to get the big pink ribbon
off his tail!

Winnie's Sat Nav

Winnie and Wilbur had just finished polishing all the cauldrons.

'All done, Wilbur!' said Winnie, having a nice stretch. 'Now we can do whatever we blooming well like!' But just then . . .

Neeeow-crump! Something flew through the window and landed beside Winnie.

'What the hiccuping heck is that?' said Winnie.

It was a message pod.

'Oooer, how modern!' said Winnie.
'I bet Wanda sent it!'

She had. Winnie pushed the button
on the pod, and heard Wanda's shriek
coming out.

'Winnie! Can you hear me?'

'Of course I blooming can!' said
Winnie, holding the pod away from her ear.

'Winnie, you've got to come and see my new abode. Wayne and I have just moved in. It's at Piddling-in-the-Puddle—ever so picturesque. It's so stylish and convenient and hygienic and up-to-the-minute and architect designed. A neat bungalow. Not like your stinky ramshackle old-fashioned mess of a place, Win! Come to tea and see it. Three o'clock. Oh, and you can bring that scraggy old cat of yours if you must.'

147

'Mrrrow!' said Wilbur.

'You're abso-blooming-lutely right,
Wilbur!' said Winnie. 'That sister of mine
is as rude as a hippopotamus's bottom.
Still, family is family. We'd better go and
see her boring new abode. We should take
a bungalow-warming present with us.'

'Mrrow?' Wilbur shrugged.

'I've no idea,' said Winnie. 'Perhaps a
nice budgie? It would have to match
her colour scheme.'

Pounce-slurp! acted Wilbur.

'Oo, yes, you're right!' said Winnie.
'A budgie wouldn't last five minutes with
that Wayne about the place! Perhaps a
vulture would be better? It could sit on her
television and sing vulture songs. Hmm.'

149

Twang-cuckoo! Twang-cuckoo!

went Winnie's watch.

'Heck, it's two o'cuckoo already! No time to get any blooming present! We must go! Er . . . where is Piddling-in-the-Puddle?' wondered Winnie.

Wilbur flapped out a big map, but . . .

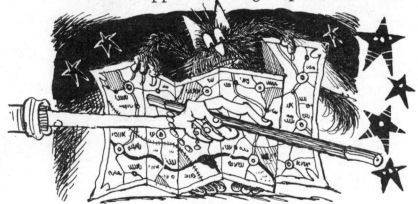

'Put that map away, Wilbur!' said Winnie. 'I'm going to show Wanda that I can be modern, too!' Winnie waved her wand. *Abracadabra!*

Instantly, there was a sat nav box on the table. Winnie stuck the box and wires onto her broom.

'Hop on board, Wilbur!' she said. Then she poked at the sat nav screen.

Bleep! Bloop-blop!

'All set!'

'Meeeow!' Wilbur rolled up his map and stuck it under his arm.

'We won't need *that*!' scoffed Winnie. 'Sat navs work like magic! Close your eyes and it'll take us where we want to go!'

So Winnie and Wilbur both closed their eyes tight.

'Go!' said Winnie, and whoosh! Up and off they flew.

'Wheeee!' said Winnie.

But soon—**clatter clatter**—Wilbur's teeth were chattering.

'It's b-b-bloooming c-c-cold,' said Winnie. 'I w-w-wonder . . .?' She opened her eyes. 'Heck in a helmet, Wilbur! Look at all those stars! We're *lost*! In *outer space*!'

154.

'Mrrrww!' said Wilbur, pointing a claw. Just ahead of them was a spaceship with a big net dangling from it.

'Space fishing!' said Winnie. 'Who? What?' But she didn't have time to wonder any more because the spaceship's net suddenly swooped around Winnie and Wilbur and the broom.

'Ooeer!' said Winnie as they were swept up in the net, tumbled through the door of the spaceship and onto the floor.

'Well!' said Winnie, untangling herself, jumping to her feet and wagging a finger. 'Just what . . . Oh!' Winnie suddenly saw who she was talking to.

155

Aliens. Lots of aliens.

'Oh. Er . . . hello,' said Winnie.

'Ploot pling pluggle!' said one
alien. It pointed at Winnie. Then all the
other aliens pointed at her, and they
laughed. **'Pli-pli-pli!'**

Then the aliens prodded Winnie.

'Oi!' said Winnie, and she hopped
to one side.

156

'**Pli-pli-pli!**' laughed the aliens.
They prodded her again until she was
jumping all over the place. The aliens were
so busy laughing that they didn't notice
Wilbur slink and prowl his way around
the edge of the spaceship until he came
to the controls.

Wilbur unfurled his map. Then he began
to poke at screens and pull levers and push
buttons until—**lurch! swerve!**—the
spaceship was suddenly whizzing through
space, heading towards Earth.

Neeeeeoow-bump! They landed.

'Pliggle?' said the aliens to each other.

'Where are we?' asked Winnie.

Wilbur pointed.

'Wanda's blooming bungalow!' said

Winnie. 'And there she is!'

'Goodness, Winnie,' said Wanda,

looking at the spaceship. 'That *is* modern.

But what are those green things?'

'Oh,' said Winnie. 'Well, they are . . . um

. . . well, aliens . . . to dance for you.'

'Pliggle?' said the aliens.

Wanda and Wayne showed Winnie
around the new bungalow. It was
yawningly tidy and dull.

'The tiles came from Italy, you know.
Wayne's silk cushions came from Iran.
The . . .'

Yawn-yawn! 'Lovely,' said Winnie.
'Now, could we have tea? I'm as parched
as parchment!'

They sat outside on the patio. 'These chairs came from . . .' nattered on Wanda. But it didn't matter because Wilbur switched on some loud music. Winnie slurped bindweed tea and scoffed raspberry bums while the aliens began to dance.

Rumpety-tiddly-tump! went the music.

Poke-poke! went Wilbur with
a wand to make the aliens dance.

Hop-hop! went the aliens.

'Hee hee!' laughed Winnie.

The aliens seemed to enjoy dancing,
and soon even Wanda was clapping along.

'Great tea party, Wanda!' said Winnie
when the dancing was finished.

'Thank you, Winnie!' said Wanda. 'But
don't go just yet, will you? The trouble
with a perfect home is that there's nothing
to do to it.'

'Oh you're as bored as an ironing board!' said Winnie. 'Why don't you keep the aliens to keep you busy!' And she shooed them inside, sliding the glass door shut.

'Ooo, mind my ornaments!' said Wanda. But it was too late.

'I'm ever so sorry, Wanda!' said Winnie. 'Quick! Get the aliens back into their spaceship, Wilbur!'

163

So Wilbur herded them back into their spaceship. **Brrrrm!** The engines fired . . . but the spaceship didn't move.

'That crash landing has broken their navigation system!' said Winnie.

Wilbur pointed to Winnie's sat nav.

'Good thinking, catman!' Winnie. stuck her sat nav onto the spaceship and pressed 'go'. 'They're off!' she said.

'I'll have to redecorate now!' smiled
Wanda happily.

'We're off too,' said Winnie. 'Bye!'

'Pling-plip!' said a tiny voice.

'What?' began Winnie.

Wanda blushed. 'I decided to keep just
one alien,' she said, lifting her hat. 'It is so
stylish, from outer space, you know . . .'

'Bye!' said Winnie. 'Let's see your map
then, Wilbur, and find our way home!'

165

Winnie Shapes Up

Snap-snap-snap-snap-snap!

went the alarm croc beside Winnie's bed.

Snip-snap!

'What? Where? Why?' Winnie opened a bleary eye. *Yawn!* 'It can't be time to get up already, can it?

Wilbur yawned wide and stretched long.

'Heck, Wilbur!' said Winnie, sitting up. 'I've had a whole night's sleep, so why am I so sluggy-sloth tired?'

Yawn! went Wilbur.

167

'You're as blooming bad as I am!' said
Winnie. 'We should be fitter than this!'

With eyes only half open, stumbling and
fumbling, Winnie reached for her clothes.
'I need to get active, and that'll make me
healthy. You have to wear special clothes
to do that.' Winnie pulled up tracksuit
trousers . . . but they got stuck halfway up
her legs. 'Heck! It's worse than I thought!'
said Winnie. 'I'm as fat as a football! Help
me to heave them up, Wilbur!' So Wilbur
heaved and Winnie heaved, and the
trousers went up, but they were so tight
Winnie's legs could hardly bend. 'And the
tracksuit top is just as blooming tight!'
complained Winnie as she wrenched the
zip upwards.

'Me-he-heow!' laughed Wilbur.

'Don't laugh!' said Winnie. 'You're as unfit as I am! We need exercise and healthy food.'

'Meeow!' wailed Wilbur.

'Well, it's no good being too tired to get up in the morning and too fat to fit our clothes,' said Winnie.

So they had just two pong berries each for breakfast. (Although Wilbur gobbled a rat when Winnie wasn't looking.)

Rumble! went Winnie's tummy. Winnie looked longingly at the biscuit barrel. 'Chocolate suggestive biscuits! Tipsy creams!' Then she shook her head. 'No!' she said. 'There isn't any room for biscuits inside this tracksuit anyway. Off we go to the gym, Wilbur!'

Gulp! went Wilbur.

171

There was a personal trainer at the gym. He was big. He was muscly. His name was Nigel.

'Flex your arm!' said Nigel. Winnie bent her flabby arm but it wouldn't flex. 'Bend and stretch!' said Nigel. Winnie bent, but she couldn't bend very far. She tried to stretch, but her tracksuit was so tight she couldn't do that very well either. 'Dear, oh dear,' said Nigel. 'You need a complete workout!'

'Me-he-heow!' laughed Wilbur.

'And so does your cat!' said Nigel. 'Go and get dressed in your sporty gear, cat!'

Wilbur came back in a cat tracksuit.

'Tee-hee!' laughed Winnie.

'Flex your arms!' Nigel told Wilbur.

Wilbur did, and—**boing!**—up popped some impressive bulges.

173

'Wow!' said Winnie. 'I never knew . . .'

'Cut the cackle and get working, Winnie!' said Nigel. 'Wilbur is already in good shape.'

So Wilbur relaxed on a lounger and watched.

'Lift those weights!' said Nigel to Winnie.

Winnie tried. **Heave! Huff-puff!** Wheeze! 'They're too blooming heavy to lift!' she said.

'No excuses!' said Nigel.

But when Nigel turned away for a moment, Winnie whipped out her wand. *'Abracadabra!'*

And instantly the weights became as light as a feather. Up-up-down! 'Easy-peasy give-someone-you-love-a-squeezy!' said Winnie.

'Oh! That's better,' said Nigel. He didn't know that Winnie had made all the weights in the gym weightless. They were so light they were starting to lift people up into the air.

'Help!' they called, hovering near the ceiling.

Nigel told Winnie to get on the treadmill.

The treadmill was boring.

'It's just walking!' said Winnie. 'I can do that at home!'

'You should be jogging, not walking!' said Nigel.

'All right, I will!' said Winnie. Out came the wand. *Abracadabra!*

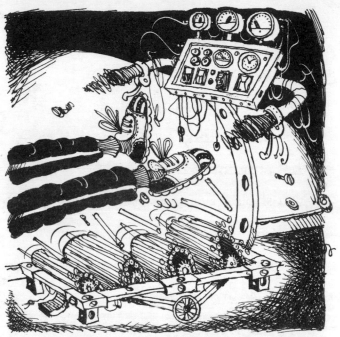

Instantly all the treadmills were going so fast they were just a blur, and people were flying off them backwards.

'Stop!' said Nigel. So Winnie stopped.

'Can I go home now?' she asked.

'No! You're going swimming next,' said Nigel.

There were people already in the pool, splashing about.

'That looks fun!' said Winnie.

'Well, it shouldn't be fun!' said Nigel. 'They should be swimming so fast it hurts!'

'Would you like me to make them go faster?' asked Winnie.

'N—' began Nigel.

But Winnie was already waving her wand.

Abracadabra!

179

Instantly there was a shark in the pool!
Everyone screamed! And they *did* swim
faster. They swam really, really fast and
then they jumped out of the pool and
they ran!

'There aren't many people left in this gym, are there?' said Winnie. 'Nigel? Nigel?'

But Nigel had run away along with everyone else.

'Just you and me, Wilbur,' said Winnie. 'I'm so hot I feel like an ice cream in an oven. Shall we have a nice cool shower and then go home?'

So Winnie unzipped her tracksuit top.
It came off quite easily now. So did the
trousers.

'Ee, I have lost weight!' smiled Winnie.
Then, 'Oh!' she said. Because she was still
wearing something—her woolly pyjamas!
'No blooming wonder the tracksuit was
tight on top of that lot!' said Winnie.
'No flipping wonder I was hot! Silly me!'

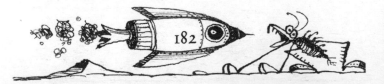

'Me-he-heow!' laughed Wilbur.

'Stop that laughing and take off your tracksuit!' said Winnie.

So Wilbur pulled off his tracksuit . . . and two oranges fell out of the sleeves.

'What?' said Winnie. 'Are those what Nigel thought were your muscles?'

Wilbur grinned.

'You naughty cat!' said Winnie.

183

·ΚΩΣΤΑΛΩΣ·
ΚΑΦΕ

As they walked home Winnie had to
hold up her tracksuit trousers to stop them
from falling down.

'I've lost so much weight and without
the pyjamas underneath I'm as skinny as a
skellington! We need to eat, Wilbur!'

'Meeow!' said Wilbur, pointing to a café.

'Good idea!' agreed Winnie.

Winnie and Wilbur ordered everything on the menu. They scoffed and scoffed until they were fit to burst.

And guess who was sitting in the café eating almost as much as they were?

'Nigel!' said Winnie. 'Would you like me to add some sour grape sauce to that lot?' She waved her wand. *Abr—*'

But Nigel was out of the café and running down the street.

'Goodness-pudness, he is keen on his keep fit, isn't he!' said Winnie. 'I don't think I could run with this lot inside me.

In fact I don't think I can . . .' **Rip!**
Winnie's tracksuit trousers split at the
bottom, showing her frilly bloomers.
'Oh, no!' wailed Winnie.

Everyone in the café began laughing and
pointing . . . and soon Winnie *was* running
down the street, after all!

Winnie's House Party

Winnie woke in the deep dark middle
of the night, clutching her tatty batty
blankets and listening to the darkness,
and wondered what had woken her.

Silence.

There should have been a sound of
Wilbur snuffling and grunting.

'Wilbur?' Winnie picked up her wand.
swish! *'Abracadabra!'* The end of the
wand glowed like a torch, which scribbled

189

light around the room. Winnie shuffled
into her slip-sloppers, pulled on her
messing gown, and set off along the long
dark landing. She felt terribly lonely,
all on her only in that big house.

'Wilbur?'

Winnie opened door after door, but the
only answer she got back from the empty
rooms was her own echo.

'Where are you?' said Winnie.

'Where are you?' said the echo.

'I'm here, you fool!' said Winnie.

'I'm here, you fool!' said the echo.

Crash!

'What was that?'

Winnie hurried downstairs to the

kitchen and shone her wand-torch . . .

'Wilbur, there you are!'

'Mnmnmeeow,' said Wilbur, licking his lips.

'Heck, Wilbur! You've cooked more than we could eat in a week!' said Winnie. 'Right, that's it!'

'Meeow?'

'We're going to have a house party!'

'Me-he-he!' laughed Wilbur.

'Not a party for houses! That would be as silly as a snail taking up clog dancing. A party for people in our house. We've got empty rooms and too much food. And I'd like people to talk to instead of just cats and echoes.'

'Mrrow!' scowled Wilbur.

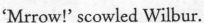

192

So Winnie raced around her house,
magicking rooms ready for guests.

'Abracadabra!'

Cobweb curtains appeared.

'Abracadabra!'

There were suddenly toad-plump
cushions, vases of thistles, slug-slime soaps
in plastic packets, and more.

'Our guests will be as snug as a whole
termite hill of bugs!' said Winnie.

'Abracadabra!' Winnie magicked
herself a magnificent party dress. 'Now we
just need to plan an itinerararerary.

'Meeow?'

'It's a list of what we'll do and when
we'll do it,' said Winnie. 'You'll have to
write it down, Wilbur.'

195

· ITINERARARERARY ·

8.00am Guests arrive. Show
them to their rooms.

9.00am Breakfast. ✦

10.00am Play hide and seek
in the garden.

1.00pm Picnic lunch ✦

2.00pm Games with bats
(from the battery)
and balls.

6.00pm Supper ✦

7.00pm Watch dVd
'Witch Upon a Star'

8.00pm Bedtime

196

'There!' said Winnie, pinning the
itinerararerary to the fridge. Her
witch-watch said it was eight o'clock
already. 'Where is everyone?' said
Winnie. 'Oh, whoops! I've not invited
them yet!'

Winnie tapped buttons on her telling
moan to call her sisters Wilma and Wanda
and Wendy, and her Uncle Owen, her
Auntie Alice, and her Cousin Cuthbert. She
invited them all to her party, and they all
texted back 'yes'. They forgot to add 'please',
which Winnie thought was rather rude. And
they all asked if they could bring friends
along with them, which Winnie thought was
even ruder. But she said, 'Oh, all right then.'

198

Bing-bong! They all arrived.

'Meet Carol,' said Uncle Owen.

'Allow me to introduce Zane, Stig, and Fang,' said Cousin Cuthbert.

'This is Clemency,' said Auntie Alice. 'I'm not sharing a room with her, mind.'

Luckily Winnie's house was big enough to have rooms for everyone, not that any

of them were happy with what they got.

'I wanted a sea view,' said Wilma.

'But we aren't anywhere near the sea!' said Winnie.

'Humph,' went Wilma.

'Can't we have bunk beds?' said Cuthbert.

'This pillow is lumpy!' said Carol.

'Oh, for goosy-gander's big fat panda's sake, let's have breakfast,' said Winnie.

It got worse at breakfast. Cuthbert said,
'You know why they call it breakfast?'

'Why?'

'Because it's when you break things,
fast!' he said. And he picked up his snereal
bowl and threw it onto the floor—**smash!**

And soon—**rip! crash! splinter!**—
Winnie's guests were having a smashing
time, breaking her things. They were
behaving very badly.

201

'Come into the garden!' said Winnie. But they went on behaving badly in magical ways. **Pow! Zip! Zap! Zlop! Zing! Croak!** Magic was flying off wands all over the place. Winnie ducked. 'Er . . .' she said, 'we must play hide and seek now. It's on the itinerararerary!'

'Bagsy I'm "it",' said Wendy. 'Everybody hide while I count to a hundred. One—tickle flea, two—tickle flea, three . . .'

Winnie's guests hid here, there and everywhere.

Winnie dug her way into the smelly compost pile of old leaves and peelings and rottings. It was soft and warm and buzzing with flies.

'This is nice!' said Winnie, settling into the quiet smelly warmth.

But, as her witch-watch ticked on,
Winnie could hear chatting and laughing.
'They've found everyone except me. Clever
me!' she said. Then it went quiet. 'Hey!'
called Winnie. She climbed out of the
compost and stomped inside . . . where her
guests were causing havoc!

Winnie was dripping with muck. Her
guests looked at her and were about to laugh
when Winnie put her hands on her hips.

'You are all so RUDE!' she shouted.

And everyone froze.

'I don't want you at my party any longer,' said Winnie. 'Go home. NOW!'

'But the itinerararerary says food and films and . . .' began Aunt Alice.

Winnie was wondering if they would all refuse to go, when . . .

Thump, thump, thump!

Winnie looked over her shoulder, and saw Jerry coming through the garden. She turned back to her guests.

'If you don't all go home now, I'll get my big brother onto you!'

'What big brother?' asked her guests (especially her sisters).

'My big brother, Jerry. Look!' Winnie pointed. 'There he is!'

Thump, thump!

'Can I borrow a cup of sugar, please, Missus?' said Jerry.

'He's big, isn't he?' said Winnie.

Winnie's guests gasped. They grabbed their bags and they tumbled out of the house and away.

'Thanks, Jerry!' said Winnie. 'Will you stay for tea?'

It was nice sitting and chatting and scrunching and slurping and burping with just Jerry and Scruff and Wilbur, with no itinerararerary and no magic.

When Jerry and Scruff went home, Winnie soaked the compost off in a nice bath of fresh frogspawn bubbles. Then she and Wilbur settled back in their own old bed as the empty house settled to silence around them.

'Goodnight, my lovely,' said Winnie.

'Goodnight, my lovely,' said her echo.

'Purrrrrr!' said Wilbur.

And that was just enough company.

Winnie's Pedal Power

Creep-creep-creep. A bush with leaves and black hair and a long nose and a strange stripy double trunk was scuttling across Winnie's garden. **Rustle-creep!**

'Tweet?' went a pretty little bird. Then, 'Meeow!' **Pounce!**

'Tweet-tweetety-TWEET!' Flip-flap-flutter!

'Wilbur, you BAD cat!' The bush wagged a twig at Wilbur. 'Were you going

to eat that pretty fountain-tailed spotted nit-catcher?'

'Mrrow.' Wilbur looked at his claws.

'Huh!' puffed the bush. 'Well, I'm going to make a bird table that is too high for you to reach, and then the birdies will be safe!' The bush waved a wand twig. **'Abracadabra!'**

And instantly there appeared a very big bird table mounted high on a greasy pole.

'Try climbing that!' said Winnie-the-bush.

Scrabble-scrabble went Wilbur. **Slip-slide. Splat-cat!**

'Hee-hee!' laughed Winnie. 'Now all the birdies in the world can come and visit me and not get pounced on.'

Back in her house, Winnie took a dusty
musty fusty old book off a shelf. It was
Great-Grandma Wilhelmina's Big Book
of Birdies. She put a tick beside the
fountain-tailed spotted nit-catcher.

'Now I want to see all those other
birdies. We need food for that birdie table.'

Winnie and Wilbur put small seeds and
ants' ankles and wasps' warts onto the bird
table, then they hid. Soon—**flippety-flap**—down came wrens and hoppit-poppets and finches and plumed plumps.
Winnie put more ticks in her Big Book
of Birdies. **Tick, tick, tick!**

'We need different food to attract different birdies,' said Winnie. So she and Wilbur got out spades and dug nice fresh wiggling worms and slithering snails and bumbling beetles.

'Num-yum!' said Winnie, trying some. 'Lucky birds!' And—**flap-flap-flump**—down came pigeons and frumples and blackbirds and screech-wimpers. Winnie put more ticks in her book.

Next they put dead critters and
snake-cake and chilli biscuits onto the bird
table. **Neeeow-flop!** Down thudded
eagles and hoot-ninnies and condors and
wobble-wings.

'Look out!' said Winnie as a great galumphing ostrich came crashing along to gobble food off the ground under the bird table. **Tick, tick,** went Winnie. 'That's all of them spotted . . . oh! Except for a dodo. Why haven't we seen a dodo?'

Winnie waited with her big pencil all ready to tick . . . but time went on . . . and on . . . and on . . . and no dodo came.

'Perhaps dodos are particular about how they eat,' said Winnie. So they hang-dangled some of these. Sprinkled some of those. They even set a table with a knife and fork. Flocks of other birds came—**squawk-peep-chirrup-kraaak-chirp-cuckoo-quack!**—but still no dodo.

It was getting cold and dark.

'Botherarmarations!' said Winnie. 'We'd better go inside and I'll cook us some spossages.'

Winnie turned on the lights and heaters and the oven and the television. And there was a woman who was just saying, 'Of course, dodos are extinct . . .'

'Dodo's stink?' said Winnie, getting excited. 'Oo, I like a good stink!'

But the telly woman went on, 'The last dodos were hunted and eaten over three hundred years ago. Now they are gone for ever.'

'Oh, no!' said Winnie. 'Poor dodos! Naughty blooming cats eating them all!'

'It was people who killed the dodos,' said the telly woman.

221

'People!' said Winnie.

But the telly woman was still talking. 'And people will make other birds and animals extinct unless we stop cutting down forests for fuel. We must use less fuel to save our lovely . . .'

Winnie jumped up. 'Turn everything off that uses power, Wilbur!'

Bop! Off went the telly. **Click!** Off
went the fire. **Snap!** Off went the lights.

'Mrrrow!' went Wilbur as Winnie stood
on his tail.

'We must save the world for the lovely
birdies and animals!' said Winnie.

223

Brrr! It was early for bed, but it was cold and dark, and they couldn't cook splossages without the oven on.

Bump! Crash! They went upstairs and jumped into bed. But Winnie stayed wide awake, thinking, and feeling hungry. Suddenly she sat up. 'I've got a blooming brilliant idea to save the birdies! Come on, Wilbur!'

Winnie and Wilbur fumbled their way out into the silvery moonlit garden.

'We need invention sorts of things,' said Winnie. They collected old wheels and chairs and cogs and chains and wires and tubes and pedals and planks and clocks.

'Stand back!' Winnie waved her wand. '*Abracadabra!*'

Clatter-CRASH! In a puff of magic, the bits all came together.

'Meeow?' asked Wilbur.

'It'll make electricity without polluting!' said Winnie. 'Hop on, let's get pedalling!'

Clank! The machine began to churn. **Zap!** Lights flickered on inside the house.

'This is brilliant!' said Winnie. **Puff! Pant!** But, 'Heck in a handbag, however will I cook those splossages in the kitchen at the same time as being out here and pedalling the power to make the oven hot? Ooo, my poor old legs are turning to soggy spaghetti. I can't keep . . . Oh!'

226

227

Suddenly, strangely, stupendously the garden was lit up with a flickering glowing light. 'Cooer!' Winnie looked around in wonder.

'Mrrow!' Wilbur pointed. A most beautiful orange traily-feathery bird was flying down through the sky.

'It's a blooming phoenix!' said Winnie. 'And it's come for the chilli biscuits I put on the bird table!'

Winnie and Wilbur got down off their contraption. They stood and watched in wonder as the huge orange-red-gold bird settled to feed on their bird table, setting the table alight so that it lit the garden like a great torch.

229

'Nice and warming!' said Winnie.

People in the village saw the fire.

'It's a bonfire party!'

Children got out of bed. The grown-ups switched off their lights and their televisions and their radios and took their children over to Winnie's house.

'Wow!' they said when they saw the phoenix. Then the phoenix began to sing a strange, wild, haunting song. Winnie drummed a beat with her wand and everyone started dancing by the light of the flames until their legs ached.

So Winnie waved her wand again.

'Abracadabra!' to turn her generator into
a massage chair for all those tired legs.

'Mine are still tired from pedalling!' said
Winnie. And she was first to try the
massage chair with Wilbur.

So because everyone in the village had come to Winnie's phoenix party, instead of sitting at home with their lights and televisions and radios on, Winnie had (sort of) saved the world.

'I'm glad we did our bit to help the animals and birdies,' said Winnie, 'even though I never did get to see a dodo.'

Winnie Minds the Baby

'What shall we do with this nice sunny day, eh, Wilbur?'

Winnie was leaning on her garden gate, scuffing her shoes in the dust and poking woodlice with her wand. 'How about a picnic? We could dangle our feet in the stinky swamp and nibble beetle bites and drink frothy pink burp-slurp pop. We could even . . .'

'Weeeaaaahh!' came a noise from

down the road.

'That sounds like you did yesterday,
Wilbur, when I stamped on your tail
because I thought it was a hairy snake.'

'Weeeaaaahh! Weeeaaaahh!'

Wilbur put paws over his ears.

'WEEEAAAHH!'

'Pickled parsnips, it's getting louder!'
said Winnie. And just then, round the
corner, came a lady pushing a pram.

'You want to get those wheels oiled,'
said Winnie.

'Oh, it's not the wheels. It's my baby,'
said the lady. 'He won't stop crying!'

'Really?' said Winnie, and she peered down at the very cross baby.

'Coochie-coo!' said Winnie.

The baby stopped mid-wail, and gawped at Winnie's witchy face, smiling at him.

'Biggle-boggle!' said Winnie, and she blew a raspberry.

Chuckle, went the baby.

'Goodness!' said the lady. 'You made him laugh! Oh, Winnie, you're a wonder with babies!'

'**Goo-goo,**' said the baby.

'That's all he can say at the moment,' said the lady. 'Just **"goo-goo"** and **"weeeaaaah"**. Oh, I'm so tired!'

'Why don't you go and have a snozzle-
snooze in my hammock?' said Winnie.
'Wilbur and I can babysit.'

'That's very kind of you,' said the lady.
'But do you know how to look after
babies? They need feeding. And their
nappies need changing.'

'Easy-peazy, squashed-worm squeezy,'
said Winnie. 'You don't need to worry
about a thing.'

So the baby's mummy climbed into the
hammock and was soon snoring happily.

'What shall we do with you?' Winnie
asked the baby. 'Shall we go for a picnic?'

'Goo!' said the baby.

Winnie hurled pickled pepper and sprout sandwiches into a basket. She added a bottle of pink burp-slurp pop and a packet of cabbage and caterpillar crisps. 'That's for you and me, Wilbur. Now, what would the baby like? Worms?' Winnie added a jar of baby pink worms. Then they set off to the park.

In the park, Winnie lifted the baby from his pram and sat him on a rug, and they ate lunch. The baby loved the juicy little worms.

'Goo-goo!'

He loved being swung by Wilbur.

'Goo-goo!'

Winnie loved swinging too. Swing-swong, swing-swong!

'**Wheee!**' went Winnie, tipping back
to make the swing go higher. Her hat fell
off. '**Wheee!**' went Winnie again. 'I'm
going to kick the clouds and see if they
bounce!' What she did kick was her shoe
up into the air so that it crashed down—
splat!—onto someone else's picnic.

'**Goo-goo!**' laughed the baby.

'Let's try the see-saw!' said Winnie. She
sat down hard on one end and catapulted
Wilbur into the air.

'**Goo-goo**,' laughed the baby. Then
suddenly, '**Weeeaaaahh!**' cried the
baby.

'Ooer,' said Winnie. She patted the baby
on the head. 'What's the matter diddums?'

'**Weeeaaaahh!**' went the baby.

'Are you hungry? Have another worm,' said Winnie. 'Thirsty? Have some burp-slurp to drink.'

Hiccup! Burp! 'Weeeaaaahh!' went the baby.

Wilbur pointed at the baby's bottom and held his nose.

'He needs a new nappy, does he?' said Winnie, making a face. 'I haven't got any. Do you think leaves and moss would do?'

It was a smelly job, but they did it.

'Weeeaaaahh!' went the baby, on and on.

'Whatever else can the matter be?' said Winnie. 'Does he need a sleep?' Winnie picked up the baby. 'I'll sing the song Great-Auntie Winifred used to sing to me when I was 'iccle:

Close your eyes, 'iccle baby,

close your eyes, 'iccle boy.

Don't be weepy, just be sleepy,

Close your eyes now, 'iccle boy.'

'Weeeaaaahh!' went the baby.

'Well, that didn't work, did it?' said

Winnie.

Wilbur held his tail over his ears.

'Perhaps he's bored,' said Winnie.

Winnie waved her wand. 'Abracadabra!'

And instantly the ducks from the pond and the squirrels from the trees came and danced for the baby.

'**Weeeaaaahh!**' went the baby.

'Oh, for grated gherkins' sake!' said Winnie. 'I wish you could talk, little baby, and TELL us what it is you DO want instead of just going "**weeeaaaahh**" to everything!'

That gave Winnie an idea. *Abracadabra!*

The baby paused for a moment. 'Er . . .
good afternoon!' he said. He looked just as
surprised as Winnie and Wilbur were to hear
real words coming out of his mouth.

'There!' said Winnie. 'No more crying, eh?
Just tell us what you need to keep you happy!'

'Well, where shall I begin?' said the baby.
He waved an arm in an expressive way, which
made him tumble over, and he couldn't get
up again. 'Dear, oh dear,' he said. 'I . . . er . . .
weeeaaaahh . . . I mean, I wish that
I could sit up properly, and walk about like
you do.'

'No problem-o,' said Winnie.
Abracadabra!

250

251

And instantly the baby was up and
running, chasing ducks and squirrels,
snatching at feathers and tails, and trying
to eat them.

'Catch the baby!' said Winnie. But the
baby was fast, even though his leaf and
moss nappy was sagging around his knees.

'Good afternoon!' he called to surprised
passers-by as he ran. Winnie and Wilbur
and the pram ran after him.

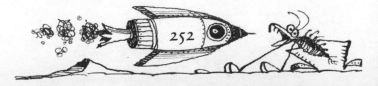

'We must give him back to his mummy,'
panted Winnie. 'Chase him over there!'

They caught the baby just as they got to
Winnie's garden gate.

'I don't want to be picked up!' said the
baby, struggling in Winnie's arms. 'Oh,
look, it's my mummy!'

Winnie could see the baby's mummy waking up. 'Quick, Abracadabra!' she said.

Instantly the baby was back to normal, but with a very surprised look on his face.

'Hello, darling!' said the lady. 'Thank you so much, Winnie. Was he any trouble?'

'Er . . .' said Winnie.

'What have you been up to?' the lady asked her baby.

'Gurgle-wurgle-boggle-boo!'

'I do believe you've taught him to talk, Winnie!' And off they went, happy.

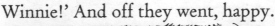

254

'Wilbur,' said Winnie, 'when DO babies say their first words? Without magic.'

'Meeow,' shrugged Wilbur.

'Well, I hope this baby forgets all about today before he learns to talk and tell his mummy about it!' said Winnie.

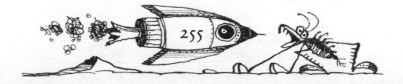

Winnie Goes for Gold

Winnie and Wilbur were wearing large
veiled hats and gloves and suits and boots.

Buzzzzzz! went the bees in a dark
cloud around Winnie. **Puff-puff!** went
Wilbur's smoke machine to make the bees
sleepy. **Cough-cough, buzz-buzz,**
went Winnie, Wilbur, and the bees.

'This is the best honey in the world!'
said Winnie. 'Collected from our own
pongwort trumpet flowers and tasting like

nothing you've ever had from a honey jar
before!'

The frames of honeycomb that Winnie
lifted dripping and dribbling from the hive
didn't look like any honey you've ever had
from a jar, either. This honey was purple,
and it fizzed.

258

'Oo, Wilbur, we can have honeyed cockroach crunch biscuits, and honey spread on nuffins, and . . . oh, I've gone and forgotten the jars, and now I've got honey dripping into my boots.'

Buzzzzzz! Bing bing!

'Eh?' said Winnie. 'Whoever heard of bees saying "bing"?'

'Meeow!' Wilbur pointed.

'Oh, it's my blooming mobile moan!' said Winnie. 'How am I meant to answer it when my hands are all sticky?'

Buzzzzzz! Bing!

'Wait a minute!' said Winnie, trying to dig out her phone at the same time as holding a frame full of sticky goo with bees buzzing all around it. She lifted the phone to her ear. 'Who is it?' she said. 'I'm buzzy. I mean busy.' There was a pause.

'Oh, it's you, Mrs P. You sound a bit
flustered.' Pause. 'Oh, I see. Mmm. Yes.'
Pause. 'I've got just what you need! Fresh
as anything! I'll just put it into something
other than my boots, and I'll be there.
Don't you worry, Mrs P. The little
ordinaries will have their honey tea!'

261

'Meeow?' asked Wilbur as Winnie tried and tried to put down the phone that was honey-stuck to her hand.

'It's school Sports Day,' said Winnie. 'They've got scones for the tea but no honey to put on them. Right, I need a good big jar. Where's my wand?' Winnie waved her wand. *'Abracadabra!'*

And instantly there appeared a big
Greek jar decorated with people running
and jumping and fighting and throwing
javelins and discuses and wrestling.

'Oo, just right for Sports Day!' said
Winnie. 'Look, Wilbur! It's the Olympic
Games. That's an extra special sort of
Sports Day from the olden days.'

Pour, lick, slurp! Buzzzzzz!

Winnie and Wilbur got the honey into the jar . . . and all over their gloves and suits . . . as the bees told them what they thought of honey thieves. **Buzzzzzz!**

'Come on!' said Winnie, trying to peel off her gloves and hat and suit at the same time as carrying the jar to the school.

Winnie and Wilbur jogged with the jar
to the school field where loudspeakers
were announcing:

'Year Three egg-and-spoon race to the
starting line, please!'

'Egg-and-spoon race!' said Winnie,
stopping still in the middle of the field.

'Ah, there you are!' said Mrs Parmar, hurrying over. 'Bring the honey to the tea tent, please.'

'But that's not right,' said Winnie. 'They didn't do egg-and-spoon races at the Olympic Games.'

'This isn't the Olympics!' said Mrs Parmar. 'Oh, good gracious, whatever . . .'

BUZZZZZZ!

The bees had caught up with Winnie and their stolen honey.

BUZZZZZZ!

'Run!' said Mrs Parmar.

Winnie ran.

She ran fast around the race track.

'Yay! Well done, Winnie!' shouted the children.

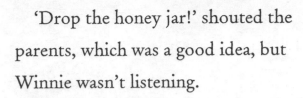

'Drop the honey jar!' shouted the parents, which was a good idea, but Winnie wasn't listening.

BUZZZZZZ!

Winnie jumped over the tug-of-war rope.

Buzzzzzz!

'DROP THE HONEY JAR!'

Winnie wasn't listening. She hurdled

over pushchairs.

Buzzzzzz!

'DROP THE . . .' But it was no good.

There was the table full of prize cups,

and the bees were getting closer every

moment! Winnie waved her wand.

'Abracadabra!' And instantly her wand became very long and bendy, so that— **boing!**—Winnie pole-vaulted right over the prizes table and the headmaster.

'Hooray!' shouted the children.

Buzzzzzz!

'DROP THE JAR!' shouted the grown-ups. But—**splash!**—Winnie landed in the swimming pool. **Paddle, paddle, paddle!** went Winnie.

'Yippeeee!' shouted the children.

Buzzzzzz! went the bees very loudly in Winnie's ears as she staggered from the pool, too tired to run any more.

'DROP THE JAR!'

And this time Winnie heard.

With an almighty effort she hurled that
jar of honey just as far as she could
... which wasn't very far at all ... and—
smash!—it became a pile of sticky
pottery pieces covered in bees.

'The honey is running away!' wailed
Winnie.

She waved her wand. *Abracadabra!*

And instantly bits of jar and dollops of honey spun into a blur, and then settled back together, looking like . . . this.

'Oh dear,' said Winnie.

'Put the jar on the table with the others,' said Mrs Parmar. 'It's time for the prizes, and then for tea.'

There were cups for this, and certificates for that. 'What about this one?' asked the headmaster, pointing at Winnie's jar.

'I believe it depicts the ancient Olympic Games,' said Mrs Parmar.

'Who has won it?' asked the headmaster.

'Winnie has,' said Mrs Parmar. 'She ran, jumped, hurdled, vaulted and swam faster and further than anybody else today.'

'HOORAY!' shouted the children.

'At the ancient Olympic Games,' explained the headmaster, 'they gave winners a crown of laurel leaves. Today they give gold medals.'

'That sounds nice!' said Winnie. So Wilbur wove her a pongwort trumpet-leaf crown. The only gold was the honey that Winnie licked from her sticky fingers.

At tea they talked about sports from the olden days.

'Throw your empty plates across the field,' said Winnie. 'See who can get them the furthest. That's what they're doing on my jar.'

Soon there were people running with cupcakes on their noses, hopping with their shopping, hurling handbags, and all sorts.

'You can see why the Olympics caught on, can't you!' said Winnie to Wilbur. She was too tired and too full of tea to do any more racing or hurling herself, but she was having fun.

That night, Winnie put her cracked and
stuck-together jar by her bed. The athletes
were still running round it. They made
Winnie feel dizzy, then dozy, then snoozy.
Snore!

She dreamed of driving a chariot pulled
by a giant Wilbur and chased by bees.

And Finally...

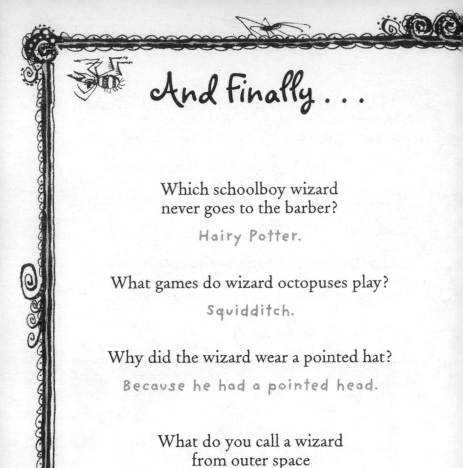

Which schoolboy wizard
never goes to the barber?

Hairy Potter.

What games do wizard octopuses play?

Squidditch.

Why did the wizard wear a pointed hat?

Because he had a pointed head.

What do you call a wizard
from outer space
A flying sorcerer.

Why aren't they making magic wands any longer?

Because they're long enough already.

What did the wizard say when he burped while playing football?

Sorry. It was a freak hic.

Why did the wizard keep turning into Mickey Mouse?

He kept having Disney spells.

Which schoolboy wizard is yellow and greasy?

Harry Butter.

When is it bad luck to have
a black cat follow you?

When you're a mouse.

What happened to the cat who
swallowed a ball of wool?

She had mittens.

What is an octopus?

An eight-sided cat.

When should a
mouse carry an
umbrella?

When it's
raining cats
and dogs.

What do cats eats for breakfast?

Mice Krispies.

How can you stop your cat from
meeowing all night in the back garden?

Put him in the front garden.

I've lost my cat.

Why don't you put an advertisement
in the newspaper?
Don't be stupid — he can't read.

How does a
witch's cat stop
a DVD?

It pushes the
PAWS button.

Why couldn't the skeleton go to the party?

He had no body to go with.

Did you hear the one about the skeleton and his girlfriend?

They broke up.

What do you call a detective skeleton?

Sherlock Bones.

What's yellow, sharp, and deadly?
Shark-infested custard.

Waiter, waiter! Do you serve children?
Only when we've run out
of everything else, sir.

What kind of soup is this?
It's bean soup, madam.
I don't care what it's been, what is it now?

Waiter, there's a twig in my soup.

Yes, madam. we've got
branches everywhere.

Waiter, there's a fly in my soup.

Don't worry, madam. that spider
on the bread will get him.

Waiter, there's a fly in my soup.

No that's the chef, sir. The last
customer was a witch doctor.

Waiter, there's a beetle in my soup.

I'm terribly sorry, sir.
We've run out of flies.

Wilbur

Winnie the Witch

Wayne

Wanda

The Shopkeeper

Uncle Owen

Mrs Parmar

Jerry the Giant

Cousin Cuthbert

Auntie Alice

Nigel

The Merman

The Little Ordinaries

The Head Teacher